THE DEVIL'S TAIL

Based on an old French legend

by Nanine Valen

illustrated by David McPhail

Charles Scribner's Sons · New York

Text copyright © 1978 Nanine Valen

Illustrations copyright © 1978 David McPhail

Library of Congress Cataloging in Publication Data
Valen, Nanine Elisabeth.
The devil's tail.
SUMMARY: Retells the traditional tale of three
brothers who find they have a most unusual visitor
in their house.
[1. Devil—Fiction. 2 Folklore] I. McPhail,
David M. II. Title.
PZ8.1.V4De   [398.2]   [E]   77-24135
ISBN 0-684-15292-4

1 3 5 7 9 11 13 15 17 19 MD/C 20 18 16 14 12 10 8 6 4 2
Printed in the United States of America

For

F.H. & A.D.

Supporters of The Hill

Preface

THERE IS a topsy-turvy town on an enormous hill in the French countryside of Burgundy where all the people talk through their noses. But this was not always the case, for at one time *Côte des Nez* or Hill of Noses, as it is now called, had no name at all. It was just a small, flat, unimportant place where everyone was only interested in himself, and people simply called it The Valley.

Some people think that The Valley became a hill during a violent earthquake many years ago. And some people say the reason that the townspeople talk through their noses is because they have come to imitate the honking of the geese that fly overhead.

But this is just not so. The truth is much stranger than that.

ONE FREEZING winter day many years ago, three brothers named Nicolas, Ernest, and Jean-François were carrying newly cut logs across the snowy fields, through the market-place, toward home. "I'm as cold as a pig's ear after the first frost," complained Nicolas, the eldest.

"Only sixty paces to go," said methodical Ernest, as they passed through the crowded marketplace, stopping for a moment to listen to the usual interesting arguments.

Old Monsieur Le Blanc was shaking his fist at Madame Pomme, the fruit seller. "Here I am, a poor old man in a wheelchair and you try to cheat me out of an apple," he shouted.

"I am certainly not trying to cheat you, you old fool," cried Madame Pomme as she checked the scale. "Two kilos of apples is what you asked for, and two kilos of apples is what I gave you. Look for yourself."

"That's just it," whined Monsieur Le Blanc. "Everyone is so exact these days. Why, when I was a boy, if you asked for two kilos of apples, they'd throw in some extras."

"Well, times have changed," said Madame Pomme. "Nowadays you get what you pay for."

"If you want to know what I think," interrupted Nicolas, who enjoyed arguing as much as any of the townspeople. But no one was interested.

"My ears are frozen," complained Jean-François, the youngest of the three brothers. "Let's move on. I think I'm going deaf."

"Only twenty-three paces left," Ernest said as they moved along to the other side of town. "Your ears look fine to me."

"Well let's make sure," said Nicolas, taking charge as usual. "Hello!" he yelled into Jean-François' right ear as loudly as he could.

"Ow!" shrieked Jean-François, jumping backward in surprise. And jumping, he stumbled. And stumbling, he fell right on top of a man who was covered with a layer of new-fallen snow and seemed to be frozen stiff. "Ohhh!" cried Jean-François as he leaped quickly to his feet. "Who is *that*?"

"It's hard to tell," said Ernest, brushing some of the snow from the man's face, "but I don't think it is anyone I've ever seen before."

"Let's bring him home to thaw out," Nicolas said, dropping his three logs and picking up the man's feet. "Ernest, put down your logs and grab the other end." Jean-François, still a bit frightened, followed the others at a distance.

When they arrived at their house, Barbotte, their mother, was sweeping the snow from the front stoop with a broom made of bound sticks. "Pile up the logs in the woodshed," she told them. Because she was not wearing her eyeglasses, Barbotte didn't notice that her sons were not carrying logs, but a frozen man instead.

The boys carried their icy package into the house, and Nicolas opened the oven door. "In he goes," Nicolas said, and they pushed the stiff man onto the heated bricks of the oven.

"He'll thaw out in there," said Jean-François when the man was safely inside.

"It should take only seven minutes in a slow oven," said Ernest.

Barbotte closed the heavy oak door against the winter wind, and shook the snow from her cape and boots. "Now don't lay eggs; make hay," she said, which was her way of telling the boys to get busy. "To begin with, you can help me find my eyeglasses." And as the boys began to hunt on top of cupboards and under beds,

Barbotte felt around the hearth for her broom. "Now where did I put that broom? Ah, here it is," she said. And she began to sweep the ashes from the hearth.

However, it was not the broom that she held in her hand, but a rather long tail which had appeared through a slot in the oven door. Indeed, the tail was so long that it did quite nicely as a broom, and Barbotte might never have noticed the difference were it not for Jean-François.

"Look what's coming out of the oven!" he shrieked. Nicolas and Ernest stopped searching for the glasses. Barbotte stopped sweeping. And they all looked.

"It's a tail!" cried Nicolas.

"At least six feet long!" cried Ernest.

"Eeek," squeaked Barbotte, dropping the tail, and peering at the slot in the oven door. "Surely that's not a cow in there?"

"Not exactly," said Ernest.

"Well, whatever it is, it's in the way. I've got to finish baking my bread," said Barbotte, glancing at the half-dozen loaves cooling on the willow ladder that hung from the ceiling.

"Let me tell you why this isn't such a good time to finish the baking…" began Ernest.

"You see," interrupted Nicolas. "We had cut our wood and walked through the marketplace with our logs, when Jean-François thought he had gone deaf and then I yelled in his ear…"

"Never mind the long story," came a deep voice from inside the oven. "Just get me out of here."

"I never thought I'd live to hear a cow talk," said Barbotte in amazement. Jean-François hid underneath the table.

"Well, it's not exactly a cow, it's more of a man," corrected Ernest.

"Then in all my days," said Barbotte, "I never thought I'd live to see a man with a tail. Who *is* he?"

"Who *am* I?" muttered the voice more to himself than to anyone else. "Is this woman stupid?"

"Yes," said Ernest, "who are you?"

"There they go again. Who do they think I am?" the voice grumbled. "Who am I? Let me out and then I'll tell you."

"No, you must tell us first," insisted Nicolas wisely.

"Oh, all right. Let's see. We'll do this the right way. Here goes":

My first letter is from A to Z.
The last four letters show how evil I can be.

"Oh dear!" said Barbotte. "He doesn't sound very pleasant, does he?"

"You wouldn't be very pleasant either," came the voice from the oven, "if you had just gone out for a short walk, had nearly frozen to death in the snow, and then had been plunged into a roasting oven."

"Well, let's find out who he is," said Nicolas. "The first letter of his name is from A to Z."

"The last four letters show how evil he can be. Maybe E-V-I-L is his last name," suggested Ernest.

"Let's start at the beginning of the alphabet. Are you Monsieur A. Evil?" asked Nicolas.

"No," said the voice.

"Then are you Monsieur B. Evil?" asked Barbotte nervously.

"*Be* Evil," chuckled the voice. "Pretty close, but incorrect," he said.

"Well, are you Monsieur C. Evil?" asked Ernest.

"*See* Evil. Not bad," said the voice. "Quite clever in fact. But wrong!"

"I've had about enough of this guessing," said Barbotte. "At this rate we'll all be here till the hens run after their eggs."

"Only twenty-three letters to go," computed Ernest.

"D is next," said Jean-François.

"D. Evil!" cried Ernest. "Wait. Wait. D-E-V-I-L. Are you the Devil, then?"

"It's a good thing *D* isn't at the end of the alphabet or I'd have been in this oven all day," muttered the Devil to himself. "Yes. Yes. I'm the Devil," he said aloud. "Now let me out!"

"Oh, dear," said Barbotte. "I never thought I'd live to see the day when I would meet the Devil. And I'm not at all sure that I want to," she concluded.

"If you *are* the Devil, we certainly will *not* let you out," said Nicolas firmly.

Now the Devil became angry. "Certainly you *will*," he shouted.

But from under the table Jean-François called, "Certainly we will *not!*"

"All right. All right. I'm not in such a hurry to get back out into that freezing weather. I'm more used to the heat than the cold in any case," said the Devil. "And I'm not unreasonable. I'll make the usual offer—the standard three wishes—but *then* you must let me out."

"It's a bargain," agreed Nicolas.

"By the time you've finished your third wish, I'll have had time to catch a good nap in here." The Devil began to enjoy the thought. "When you're ready to wish, you must tug gently on my tail to get my attention...in case I should doze...zzz...off...."

"Are you sure we couldn't let him out right now?" complained Barbotte, using the Devil's tail to whisk away more ashes from a corner of the hearth. "I wish to finish my baking."

"Done," said the Devil, awaking with a start. "Wish number one." And six steaming loaves appeared beside the first six on the willow ladder.

"Oh, good Lord," exclaimed Barbotte.

"Not exactly," said the Devil.

"Oh, dear," said Barbotte remembering, but still not quite believing who he was.

"Now you've used up one of our wishes!" complained Jean-François.

"We'll have to be careful," said Nicolas.

"Only two to go," calculated Ernest. "What shall we wish for?"

"How about a bicycle?" suggested Jean-François.

"No," said Ernest. "We would have to wish for three bicycles. And I'm not sure," he continued, "if we could wish for all three bicycles in one wish or if we would have to use three wishes. And since we only have two…"

"How about a sled?" Jean-François cried.

"A sled?" wondered Ernest.

"Wonderful!" agreed Nicolas. "It'll take only one wish, and we'll all be able to fit on."

"We'll slide and slide, we'll glide and glide…" sang Jean-François.

"Now, wait a minute," said Nicolas cautiously. "Are we sure this is what we want?"

"Yes," shouted Jean-François, impatient to be on with the wishing.

They both looked at Ernest. "It's fine with me," he said.

"Then it's settled. We wish for a sled," said Nicolas in a loud and confident voice. The boys looked around. There was no sled to be seen.

"What's the matter?" asked Jean-François. "Didn't he hear us?"

"He's probably sleeping," said Ernest. "Remember, he said we must pull on his tail." Jean-François reached for the tail.

"Wait a minute!" said Nicolas. "Let's do it together—and maybe we'll get a very big sled. Put your hands on top of mine," he directed as he grasped the tail, "and when I pull, wish for the sled as hard as you can." And that's what they did.

"Ow! Ow! Ow!" shrieked the Devil. "How's a Devil supposed to nap around here? I said pull *gently*. Now… it's a sled you want…." There was a brief pause in his grumbling. The Devil's voice rumbled low and deep. "Done," he said. "Wish number two." And there in the center of the room was the biggest, reddest sled ever made.

"Oh, dear," said Barbotte. "I suppose he really may be the Devil after all."

"Of course he's the Devil," said Jean-François with delight as he climbed onto the sled.

"Let's take it outside in the snow and try it out," said Nicolas. And so they went out again into the blustery day.

"Let's go," said Nicolas climbing on first.

"We're off!" shouted Jean-François.

"No we're not," said Ernest, who did not bother to climb on at all. "There's no hill."

"No hill?" asked Jean-François and Nicolas.

"No hill," repeated Ernest. "We forgot that there was no hill."

"Well, let's try anyway," urged Jean-François as he tried to push the sled with his feet. But the sled wouldn't budge.

"He's right, you know," admitted Nicolas, getting off the sled.

"I knew we should have been more certain before we wished," said Ernest.

"It's too late now," said Nicolas. "We'll just have to figure something out."

"We could wish for a boat," suggested Jean-François. "You don't need a hill for a boat."

"No, but you need water, and all the ponds around here are frozen," said Ernest.

And so they tried to think of something else. After a few moments, Nicolas shouted, "I've got it! We'll wish for a hill."

"Perfect," said Ernest. "A hill's all we need."

The boys raced into the house pulling the sled behind them and tracking snowy footprints across the kitchen to the oven door where the snow melted into a small pool of water around the Devil's tail.

"Give us a hill!" they panted. Plopping down on the sled, Jean-François gave the tail a good hard yank.

"Ow! Let me out!" bellowed the Devil.

"First our hill," Nicolas insisted stubbornly, sitting down on top of Jean-François.

"*Then* we will let you out," said Ernest, jumping on behind the other two.

"It's a hard bargain they drive in Burgundy," said the Devil with a groan, "but a bargain *is* a bargain," and his voice sounded like thunder as he pronounced their final wish. "One hill. Wish number three."

And as he said three, there was a great rumbling, the house shook, and the sled shot out the open door with the three boys on it.

"Let me out! Let me out!" cried the Devil, but the sled was already on its way down the hill. And what a hill it was! Never in all of Burgundy had anyone seen such a hill. It was smooth, not rough and rocky as some hills are. It had a series of gentle curves and was covered by a layer of glistening snow—just right for sledding. And the size!

Nicholas gasped as they flew down the hill. "It's enormous!" he cried.

"It's gigantic!" exclaimed Ernest.

"It's perfect!" sighed Jean-François. And for just that moment it did seem perfect. Smoothly they glided over the crest of small rises, and down they swooped on the other side. The snow blew in their faces, giving their cheeks a red polish.

But soon it became apparent that something was very wrong. The trees seemed to be growing at strange angles. "Watch out!" shouted Ernest, as an old wooden apple cart came whizzing down the hill, apples spilling in all directions. And that was only the beginning.

Down the hill rolled just about everything in town that could move—pears and potatoes, squashes and beets. And eggs! Hundreds of them rolled out of the hens' nests and splattered their way down the hillside, painting yellow splashes on the snow. Then came carts and wagons, balls and wheels, chairs and beds. And behind all this tumbled nearly everyone in the village.

"My whole fruit store… gone!" shrieked Madame Pomme, as she slid along scooping up apples and pears into her apron.

"My kitchen table!" cried Monsieur Le Blanc, as his wheelchair hit a bump.

"All my logs for the winter!" yelled Monsieur du Bois, the woodcutter, rolling behind his logs.

"Watch out!" shouted Barbotte from her whizzing rocking chair as it nearly collided with Madame Bon Bon in her bed. And as Nicolas steered a wild and unsteady course through the fruits and vegetables, tables and logs, carts and wagons, balls and wheels, chairs and beds, *and* people, the boys began to feel that perhaps they might be responsible for all the trouble.

"Things are not working out the way they should at all," said Nicolas as the sled finally plowed into a pile of potatoes and people at the bottom of the hill.

"And just how *should* things have worked out?'' demanded Monsieur Renard, the schoolmaster.

"Well, it's just that we wanted a hill to sled on,'' said Nicolas.

"Aha! So you know something about this *hill?''* cried Madame Pomme, glaring over her glasses at the three boys.

And so the boys explained how the Devil happened to be trapped in their oven—and how they were to pull his tail in order to get the wishes he had granted them in a bargain for his freedom.

"You mean that given a chance to wish, you wished for a sled and a hill?" exclaimed Monsieur Renard.

"But you see, a sled is not much use without a hill," said Ernest logically.

"A sled and a hill are not much use at all," said Monsieur Le Blanc.

"And what did you think would happen to our town when it turned into a hill?" thundered Monsieur Renard.

"And what did you think would happen to my fruit stall when all the stands were slanted downhill?" Madame Pomme said tearfully.

"You were just thinking of yourselves," said Monsieur Renard.

But Barbotte parted a mound of potatoes and apples with one great shove and stood before the boys to try and defend them. "No," she said. "They just weren't thinking at all."

"Well, let's not stand here all day. Everybody take something back up the hill," said Madame Pomme with a burst of enthusiasm. And she began to pick up her apples from where they lay scattered in the snow.

And so all of the villagers, carrying their own possessions, began to climb the long hill. And as they climbed, they saw that nothing was where it belonged. The marketplace was only a pile of fallen boards and brightly colored awnings spread out over the ground like fallen flags. Doors swung crookedly on their hinges or stuck in the door frames so that many villagers were forced to climb into their houses by the windows. In one house they saw that Madame Bon Bon's cow had wandered in from the pasture and was calmly munching her bedroom curtains.

44

The chimneys were pointing at all sorts of odd angles, causing the smoke to curl along the ground and cover everyone in a dense, smoky fog so that they could hardly see.

"*Something* has got to be done!" coughed Monsieur du Bois, stumbling into Madame Bon Bon.

"Something has *got* to be done!" sneezed Madame Bon Bon, bumping into Madame Pomme.

"Something has got to be *done!*" wheezed Madame Pomme, dropping her apples which rolled down the hill again.

"Where did you say that Devil was?" demanded Monsieur du Bois. "I've got a few wishes of my own."

"In the oven," said Jean-François. "But wait…" he called after Monsieur du Bois, who was already running toward the boys' house at the top of the hill.

"Listen…" yelled Nicolas, but by this time all the villagers were running after Monsieur du Bois.

When the boys reached home, their kitchen was so crowded that people were standing in the doorway or peering down the chimney in the hope of seeing the Devil in the oven.

"I want a new fruit stand!" shouted Madame Pomme.

"Pull the tail!" yelled Monsieur du Bois, throwing the tail over his shoulder.

"More cows!" screamed Madame Bon Bon, grabbing the tail, too.

"Down with the hill!" shouted everyone. And so as they pulled and pulled, screaming their demands, the tail stretched and stretched and stretched, and the Devil became angrier and angrier.

"There'll be the Devil to pay for this!" he cried, as more and more people grabbed onto the ever-lengthening tail, shouting wish after wish.

"No, stop!" cried Nicolas, Ernest, and Jean-François. "You don't understand." And they reached out to pull some of the people away from the tail. But suddenly, there was a snap and the tail came off! Nicolas, Ernest, and Jean-François fell over and the villagers tumbled on top of them. The oven door flew open, and out sprang the Devil.

Looking very strange without his tail, the Devil surveyed the fallen villagers, struck a dramatic pose, and declared:

> *Three wishes I gave you*
> *And this presupposes*
> *You'd not ask for more*
> *Or you'd land on your noses.*

And this is exactly what had happened. When the tail snapped, everyone fell over, squashing their noses flat.

"Nasty place," said the Devil. "Greedy, nasty place. What's the name of it?"

"It doesn't have a name," said Nicolas in a strange honking voice that didn't sound a bit like him.

"No namc, eh? Well, it has now," said the Devil.

A nameless valley until today
was Hill of Noses or Côte des Nez.

"Hill of Noses?" said Ernest in a funny voice that seemed to be coming through his nose. "Why Hill of Noses?"

"Just look at one another," said the Devil. "And listen."

"Our noses are all squashed!" cried Jean-François.

"You mean to say that our noses will always be this way?" asked Ernest.

The Devil struck another one of his dramatic poses.

Hill of Noses you shall be
until this tail grows back on me.

And with those words he was gone.

"If you ask me," said Barbotte, as she rubbed her nose, "I'd rather have a town without a name where everything is normal, than a town with a name where everything is topsy-turvy. It's such a terrible mess!"

"Don't worry, Mama," said Nicolas. "We'll help put it together somehow."

"How is my bed ever to get back up the hill again?" cried Madame Bon Bon.

"We can put it on the sled!" said Nicolas.

"You could do that?" asked Madame Bon Bon, surprised and pleased.

"Surely!" said Jean-François. "We can bring lots of things back on our sled."

And suddenly the idea caught on. Nicolas helped Monsieur du Bois carry his logs up the hill. Monsieur du Bois helped Madame Pomme build a new fruit stand, and Jean-François helped her set up the awnings. Ernest helped Madame Bon Bon pull her cow out of the bedroom, and Barbotte helped her make new curtains because the cow had completely chewed up the old ones.

And by the time the year had passed, the topsy-turvy town was back to something like normal, although still on a slant. In fact, most people thought it was better than ever. Monsieur Le Blanc came whizzing by on his wheelchair. "You can have the next ride!" he shouted to Barbotte, who had stopped to buy fruit at Madame Pomme's new fruit store. Jean-François, Nicolas, and Ernest were sledding close behind him. "We'll hitch him onto the sled and pull him back up," called Jean-François to his mother.

"That does look like fun," said Barbotte. "I wonder how long we'll be able to enjoy life on our hill?"

"What do you mean by that?" asked Madame Pomme, weighing out the fruit, and putting in an extra pear for good measure.

"Well," said Barbotte, looking out over the snowy farms and fields in the valley below, "I was just wondering when the Devil's tail will grow back, for when it does, you know we shall have no more hill."

"Yes, you're right of course," said Madame Pomme as she watched the geese swooping overhead. "You know, I've grown rather fond of our Hill of Noses. Now I'm used to our noses this way, and we never had such a beautiful view before."

"Well, it probably takes a long time to grow such a long tail," said Barbotte hopefully. "Perhaps the Devil will forget about us entirely."

And so far, at least, it seems that he has.

Notes

"To pull the Devil by the tail" (*"tirer le Diable par la queue"*) is a French expression which means to be hard-up—to have to stretch to make ends meet. The phrase is founded on a legend that is a part of French folklore. The essential elements have been preserved in this story: someone discovers the Devil frozen on a path, thaws him out in the oven, pulls his tail for material gain, attracts the attention of the greedy who do likewise, and all are punished by falling on their noses.

A version of this story is told by Charles Thuriet in his *Traditions populaires de la Haute-Saône et du Jura.* (Emile Lechevalier. Paris. 1892.) In Thuriet's version, a woodcutter finds the Devil frozen on a path. Thinking he is some poor drunkard, he brings the Devil home to his wife who thaws him out in the oven. When a scorched red tail appears through a crack in the oven door, the couple realize their advantage and pull on the tail to extract gold and other material things. Their good fortune attracts the attention of four greedy Capuchin monks who pull the tail off and fall flat on their noses. This story is also used to explain the nasal tones of the Capuchins.